Written by
Claire Mills

Illustrator
Irina Levina

Give us your feedback about this book:

amazon.co.uk

amazon.com

amazon.ca

Princess Darla was not a usual princess. She was brave and strong. Darla enjoyed archery, tree climbing, and getting muddy. She enjoyed riding Sunbeam, her unicorn.

"If only we could go outside the palace grounds," she told him one day. "I would be able to have proper fun then."

The queen was worried. "When will she learn to behave like a proper princess?" she sighed. But the king was pleased with his daughter, saying, "That's my girl!"

One day, a messenger rushed into the royal dining room. "The dragon has escaped, and the people are in danger!" he cried. "They ask your help, Your Majesty."

The king had a sad look on his face. "I'm too old for this," he said. "Wouldn't it be great if we could have a son...."

Princess Darla stood up and said, "You don't need a son; Sunbeam and I will save the people."

"Oh, Darla!" cried the queen. "What if you get attacked by armed men on the way?"

"Not to mention the dragon himself," said the king. But Darla was brave, and the king and queen later agreed to let her go. She took some food with her, as well as her bow and arrows. She climbed on Sunbeam and took off at full speed.

Sunbeam and Darla soon arrived at a village where they stopped for a drink of water.
"Look, look!" the children exclaimed as they ran out of their houses. They'd never seen a unicorn, let alone a princess. The children gathered around them.
"Can we ride him?" one of the children asked.
"Does he fly?" another asked.
Darla exclaimed, "No! He's too young to fly yet....
We must leave now to protect you from the dragon."

Sunbeam and Darla continued their journey.
They walked into a large, dark forest.
"Slow down, Sunbeam," Darla said.
"You don't want to trip over any large objects."

The road began to climb upward.
It was a hot walk, but the air was still fresh.
"That doesn't look good," Darla said, pointing to
a dark cloud in the sky. "There will be a storm."

It wasn't long before the rain began to fall heavily. There was a crack of thunder, and lightning lit up the whole sky.
"Quick, let's find some shelter," said Darla.
But something was wrong; Sunbeam was limping.

Suddenly, Darla became aware of movement in the valley below. It was large and green and had a swishing tail. "It's the dragon!" she exclaimed. "He's on his way to the village."

"Sunbeam, what are we going to do? We'll never make it down there in time even if you could gallop." Sunbeam was not going to give up so easily. With a loud whinny, he lifted his legs into the air, and they were suddenly flying—over the treetops, over the houses, and over a rainbow. Darla exclaimed, "Oh, Sunbeam! You can now fly!"

But her joy was fading. The dragon had seen them and was doing his best to hit them with his massive tail. But Sunbeam quickly dodged out of the way.

Darla took out her bow and arrows. She focused on her target and fired. The arrow hit the dragon in the neck, and he fell to the ground with a loud thud.

The villagers rejoiced as they ran out of their houses. "Long live the princess!" exclaimed the crowd. They held a big party, and everyone came. The queen exclaimed, "I'm so proud of you." "I couldn't agree with you more," the king said, winking at Darla.

Printed in Great Britain
by Amazon